I0608271

Buck & The Boy

Marco Mcdewey

Table of Contents

Dedication

This book is dedicated to my dearly departed father (Buck) and mother (Doe)

Thanks for the inspiration and guidance throughout this life.

Chapter One

It was the last day of September. I was turning thirteen in October and was looking forward to finally becoming a teenager. It seemed as if manhood was around the corner. I had just returned home from school, and the first thing I had to do was to get my chores done. I picked up the two big bags of garbage and headed toward the back gate that opened into the alley where the garbage bins stood. As I approached the gate, I could hear some rummaging amid the garbage cans. I heard grunts and snorts, almost bear-like. But my family lived in a small town in the desert, where bears weren't common. I thought maybe this was a cougar or a coyote. I opened the back gate slowly. I could see the garbage cans shaking back and forth and heard the sounds of a hungry animal. Quietly I set the bags down and picked up a big stick that lay on the ground by the gate. I edged toward the garbage cans, close enough so that I could touch one can with the stick. I reached out and gave the garbage can a slight thump. The sounds stopped suddenly as if whatever was inside was waiting for something else to happen. So again, I hit the garbage can a little harder this time. There was a sudden burst of energy as the animal jumped out of the can to land on all fours! That startled me so much that I dropped the stick and froze. The beast stood there, staring me right in the eye. I took a step back, only to trip over my stick and land with a thud on my backside. I studied the animal, realizing quickly that it was a dog. Thrown off balance as I was by this jack-in-the-box surprise, I was not really frightened of the creature. I had never met a dog that didn't like me, nor had I ever met a dog that I also didn't like. After all, a dog spelled backward is God, so what could be better than that?

The dog stared at me with his dark eyes. His ears were pulled back, teeth bared in a snarl, and the hair on his neck bristled. I could tell he was a mangy old dog without a collar and probably no home. He had a slightly matted black and brown coat. He was scrawny to the point where you could see his ribs; even the bones at his hip protruded slightly. I grabbed the stick, keeping it between him and myself, and got slowly to my feet. His eyes followed my actions as if trying to intimidate me. I wasn't scared, only cautious. Raising my left hand, I waved the stick at him, "Go on, get!" I directed. He turned quickly and scampered away down the alley. I looked in the garbage can to see what he had been after and saw an old stew bone from the dinner my mother had made a few nights ago. Meanwhile, the dog had stopped some distance away, and he now turned back to look at me as if to say, "I'm watching you, and I'm not scared of you." I lifted the bone out of the can and tossed it in the air toward the dog so that it landed a few feet in front of him. Ever so cautiously, he walked up to the bone; having sniffed at it a few times, he picked it up and scurried off down the alley as I watched him disappear from sight. Finishing my garbage duty, I went back inside the house to wash up for dinner.

My name is Dustin, and I am the youngest of four boys. I have two stepbrothers, Tony and Dell, and Bryce is my real brother. Growing up in a family of boys, I learned a lot from watching my older brothers. I learned what mistakes to avoid and also how to get away with the ones I made. My brothers were mischievous and were constantly getting into trouble.

Although I was a short-legged, slightly chubby child, I could run faster than the wind and jump higher than a kangaroo. I was considered smart and witty, and I loved a practical joke; my mother always said I was the comedian in the house.

Two weeks went by, and I thought nothing more of the animal that I had the encounter with. One Monday morning, like on every school day, my brothers and I were walking to school. My brothers went to a different school on the other side of town, but my school was only a few blocks away from home. Mother always packed a healthy lunch for us, usually a snack, a piece of fruit, and a sandwich or two. One day on my way to school, I took a shortcut that required going through an alley. About halfway down the alley, a few garbage cans were tipped over, and I could see a pair of hind legs and a tail sticking out of one can. It was that old dog again! I could tell from the color and slightly matted texture of his coat; I just knew it was him! I almost turned back and went in a different direction, but then realized I would be late to school if I did that, so I decided to proceed cautiously and slowly and try to sneak by him. I approached the garbage can slowly, trying to tiptoe past unnoticed. But one wrong step and he heard me and came flying out of the can. He spun around, growling at me again with his hair standing on end as if determined to protect the garbage can and the treasure inside from me. I could not help but laugh inside because it was almost comical. I backed slowly away from him, talking in a low, soft voice, "Good dog. Good dog." He never took his eyes off me as I knelt down on one knee, opened my lunch box, pulled out one of the Bologna sandwiches my mother had made for me, and held it out for him. "Good boy, come here. Good boy, I've got a snack for you." He took a few steps toward me, still bristling nervously. Then he sniffed the air and stopped; he wasn't coming any closer. He started growling at me again, so I tore the sandwich in half and tossed one of the halves right at his feet. He sniffed at it and gobbled it up in one bite. I don't think he even tasted it. I could tell he was malnourished, as he was obviously very skinny, and his ribs stuck out even more now than the last time I had seen him. I was already late for school, so I tossed him the other half of my sandwich also and hurried on my way. He gobbled up that half just as fast as the first one. As I approached the end of the alley, I turned to look at him one last time before he went back to what he had been doing. I felt that the sandwich I had shared with him was a peace offering between us to show that I never meant him any harm. I only wanted to pet him and be his friend.

It was now October; only two more weeks, and I would finally be thirteen, a teenager. I could not wait to have more freedom, stay up later, and be able to hang out with my friends. I hoped that Mom and Pop would get me a shotgun for my birthday. I loved to go dove and quail hunting. My dad used to say that I was his bird dog sometimes when he went hunting, and the best one he ever had. I don't know if dad knew this, but I was proud of that title. My dad was my hero. I looked up to him in every way. Wherever he went, I wanted to go too, whether it was just going to the store or going deer hunting, fishing, etc. It did not matter; I just wanted to be with him and be his little buckaroo. That is what he used to call me. My other brothers were older and had very little desire to hang out with our father; they took no interest in what he was doing. I tell you, looking back on my childhood, the best part of it was being with my dad. He taught me so much, not just about fishing and hunting but about life. I did not know it at the time, but he was preparing me for my future, for my own family, and to be a good man like him.

It was a Friday, the day that kids lived for because the weekend was just around the corner. The school day was over, and I was on my way home. I could smell dinner cooking as I approached the house. I arrived home about twenty minutes before my dad got there and ran into the kitchen to help my mom. I was her little taster and more than happy to taste anything that she had cooking, for my mother was a great cook. This day she had made a special meal which consisted of a big pot of pinto beans with cornbread and slices of white onions, the yummiest meal ever. Dad finally walked in, and even he commented on how good the food smelled. We all sat down for dinner and finished off the night with some games and TV, then went to bed. I could not wait to wake up to rule the next day—Saturday! Who knew what adventures awaited me?

Chapter Two

I woke up early that morning. The sun was just coming up, and it was going to be another beautiful, sunny day. With sleepy eyes, I made my way to the kitchen to get something to eat. I poured myself a bowl of cereal, then proceeded to the living room and sat on the couch watching cartoons until about ten o'clock. Fully awake now, I decided I would go hang out at the canal for a while, maybe catch some crawdads. When they are boiled and dipped in butter, they are so delicious. I could probably eat my weight in them, and where we lived, there was a seemingly endless supply. Mom and Pop would be up soon, but they knew that if my bike was gone, I'd be out fishing. So I grabbed a bucket, some string, and some fresh chicken liver and headed down to the canal. When I arrived at the canal, I picked out a good spot and sat down on the edge of the bank. In no time at all, I had filled about a quarter of the bucket with scrumptious crawdads. I was just rebating my line when I looked up and saw him again; there he was, that same old mangy dog.

This time he seemed even worse for wear than the last time we had met. But then, I suppose making a meal out of whatever you find in a garbage can can't be all that great.

He had not seen me yet, so I remained motionless so as to not draw attention to myself. I watched as he started to walk into the wooded thickets just off the canal road. I then stashed away my line and bucket and started to follow him as quietly as I could. I wanted to see where he was going, so although I kept my distance, I was careful not to let him out of my sight. But then, in the blink of an eyelid, it seemed he was gone! 'Where did he go?' I wondered. There was no way I could have lost him.

I walked quietly over to the spot where I had last seen him standing. What I found was a big hole in the ground. Could he be in there? I knew coyotes live in dens in the ground, but a dog? Was this even possible? I looked closer and could see his tracks at the entrance, but I was not about to crawl in there and come face to face with a mean, old dog. I looked around and could see the remains of garbage around this den, probably remnants of meals he had brought home. I slowly made my way back to the canal to resume my crawdad catching. Now that I knew where he lived, I could come back and visit him anytime.

The bucket was about three-quarters full when I ran out of bait. Pop had taught me that the best bait for crawdads is chicken liver—they love the stuff. I would tie a chunk to the end of a string and toss it in the water right next to a hole on the side of the canal bank. The crawdad would grab the liver with its claws and start eating it, and that was when you slowly pulled them onto dry land. They would get so busy eating the liver that they wouldn't even know I was pulling them out of the water, and before they knew it, they were in my bucket.

I hopped on my bike, with the bucket hanging from the handlebars, and headed home. Mom and dad loved crawdads almost as much as I did. Mother and I cleaned, boiled, and peeled the crawdads until we had a heaped plate for all of us at dinner time, and they were gobbled up in no time. Dad looked at me as he stretched back in his chair, rubbing his belly, and said, "Good job, boy." After dinner, we all went into the living room and watched some TV until it was time for bed. I flopped upon my bed and bundled up. Shutting my eyes, I started thinking about that poor old dog and how he had to live. At that, I got out of bed and went on my knees to say a prayer, "Please, god bless that mangy dog that he may someday find a home, amen." I got back into bed then and closed my eyes, and was soon fast asleep.

Chapter Three

Sunday morning, I was awakened by my mother's gentle voice. "Time to get up, boys," she said softly so as to not startle us. It was church day, so we would all put on our Sunday best and head for Sunday school. As the sermon started, we would be sitting in the big hall where the preacher and others give long talks. I did not understand most of it, as this was for the older folks. I just sat next to my mother as she listened to the lessons while scratching my back to keep me calm and quiet. We sang a few songs together, and although I could not read most of the lines, I would hum through the parts I did not know. I loved singing along with my mother; her voice was like an angel's. After the last song, it was time for me to go to Sunday school. I remember that day well, as the lesson our teacher taught us was about being kind not only to our fellow brothers but also to strangers and animals and, indeed, all of God's creatures. We are all on this earth together, and it is our job to help make it a better place for everyone.

I really took that lesson to heart as I thought to myself, whom could I help? Everyone I knew seemed fine, and I was already nice to them. I kept thinking about this after the lesson, and then suddenly it came to me! The Sunday school teacher had said all God's creatures, so what about that poor dog I had prayed for last night? If anyone needed help, it was that mangy old dog. I decided then that I would try to help him and be his friend.

We arrived home from a church full of the spirit, but with empty bellies, so mom started fixing us some dinner. On Sundays, we would eat dinner early, usually about three in the afternoon, so if one got hungry later in the day, you had to fend for yourself. I guess it was mom's day to rest, as well as the Lord's. This Sunday, mother had fixed a big pan of fried potatoes, green beans, and a pork loin on the BBQ; it was so delicious, as always. I helped clear the dinner table, and as I did, I was able to pocket some of the scraps of meat and potatoes. After dinner, I headed down to where the old dog lived. As I pedaled down the alley, I spotted an old dog dish that someone had tossed in the garbage. I picked it up and hurried on my way.

When I arrived, he was not there, so I placed the bowl by the entrance to his den and placed the meat and potatoes in the dish and then backed away about ten feet, sat, and waited for him to return. An hour went by before he showed up; the sun was just starting to set.

As he approached the dog dish cautiously, I said, "Well, it's about time you showed up for dinner." His head turned, and his back bristled again, but this time he did not growl at me.

He turned his attention back to the dish, sniffed at it, and started eating as fast as he could. I said to him, "You're a hungry boy, ain't ya?"

As he ate, I thought to myself, how did you get in this condition? How come you don't have a boy to love you? He finished licking the bowl, and I tossed him the few scraps of meat I still had left. He ate them as quickly as I could toss them out. I would toss each piece a little closer to myself to draw him in. When I was almost out of scraps, he was about five feet away and staring right at me. His eyes were a golden brown, and his coat was a brown and black mix; he seemed to be gazing right into my soul. As he looked at me, I said to him, "I'm going to call you Buck," and I tossed him the last piece of meat, which he caught in the air. Then I said I have to go home now, but I'll see you tomorrow. Slowly I stood up and walked away, and this time he was the one watching me until I disappeared from his sight. When I arrived home, mother asked, "Where have you been all night, son?" I said I was down by the canal playing, which was not a lie, as the thicket Buck lived in was right by the canal.

I did not want my parents to know about him just yet. I was an animal collector, see? At least that's what my mom and dad had said to me more than once, with my having brought home frogs, snakes, cats, lizards, bugs, and just about anything I could fit into my lunch box. Dad used to teasingly call it my bug box, which wasn't far from the truth. The dogs I would bring home were usually neighbors', and I always had to take them back. They would never let me keep any of the animals I had found; it was always the same old line, take that back outside and let it go. I did not want this to happen with Buck; I needed to find a way to properly introduce him to the family.

Chapter Four

Over the next few days, I would visit Buck every day
after school. As soon as the bell rang, I'd run like the wind
to get to my bike and pedal as fast as my little legs could
work. Every day I would save for Buck one of the
sandwiches that mother made for me. When I arrived at his
den, he was always there to meet me, and on the third day of
this routine, he was wagging his tail in delight—I could tell
he liked being loved and having a boy of his own.

Thursday morning came, and it was time to head off to
school. As I walked outside, I found Buck sleeping on our
front porch. I shooed him quickly to the side of the house

before mother came out to wave me on my way. "Stay here, boy, just for a minute." He sat down as if he understood what I was saying. At that point, mother walked out on the porch and waved to me, saying, "I love you, son, have a good day at school." I waved back to her and strode off down the street. No sooner had she gone inside and closed the door than Buck came flying around the corner of the house. He followed me all the way to school.

When I arrived at school, the playground was filled with kids playing and running. The bell rang, and I made my way to class. Buck wanted to follow me, so I turned to him and said, "No, boy! You can't come; you need to go home." He sat down then, looking at me with disappointed eyes as I turned and hurried off. The school day seemed to be over almost as soon as it had begun, and tomorrow was Friday. I ran straight to my bike, hoping that buck would be waiting for me to walk me home, but he was not there. I had told him to go home, so I rode my bike over to his den. There he was, lying down and wagging his tail with excitement as I approached. I sat down next to him while opening my lunch box, and I said, "I have a good treat for you today." Mom had made buffalo sandwiches, my favorite. Buffalo sandwiches are not made from buffalo but are actually meatloaf, but for some reason, I thought it was buffalo for the longest time. I am not sure where I picked up this notion, but one day mother asked me what I wanted for dinner, and I said buffalo. Father went to the store and bought some buffalo, mother fixed dinner, and as we all sat down to eat, I asked what it was. Father said it's what you asked for, buffalo. I looked at them in disappointment and said, "that's not buffalo." This was very puzzling to mother and father, and they fixed meal after meal for me trying to figure out what I meant by buffalo. They just wanted to know what I wanted until they finally gave up. Then one night, my mother made meatloaf. We all sat down to eat, and when I looked down at my plate, I threw my hands in the air in excitement and yelled, "yummy buffalo!" My parents laughed as the mystery was solved.

Buck and I shared the sandwich. When it was all gone, he looked up at me and rested his head on my leg. He had never done this before, but it felt good. I knew that he now loved me as I did him. I sat there with him, petting him and talking to him until the sun started to go down, at which point I got up and said, "I have to go home now." He lay there on the ground like I was still there next to him. I made my way to my bike and slowly peddled home.

The next morning I went to school as usual. When I came out on the porch, there was no dog waiting for me today. The day seemed to be long and tedious; I could not wait for the twelve o'clock bell to ring. During lunch, I was playing on the monkey bars, pretending I was a trooper in the jungle, swinging on a rope over a canyon, when a bigger kid knocked me off. I fell to the ground and landed face-first with a mouth full of sand. Now, being a smaller boy, I did tend to get picked on sometimes, but I was also a tough little guy and stood my ground. Remember, I had three older brothers who I had to fight with all the time. I went over to the bully, and like a commando, I hooked my leg behind him and grabbed him by the chest, and pushed him back. As he fell over and landed on his butt, I ran as fast as I could back to class. I could hear the laughter as I disappeared back into the classroom in a cloud of dust.

The three o'clock bell rang, a joyful sound announcing the end of yet another school day. As I got up from my desk, my teacher, Mr. Deter, asked if I could stay a bit. I slowly sank back into the seat until all the students had left. Mr. Deter then approached my desk. "You seemed somewhat preoccupied during class," he said and wanted to know if there was a problem at home or something. A somewhat slender man with a beard, about twenty-nine years in age, Mr. Deter was dressed in khaki pants and a blue button-up shirt. He was a very good teacher and got along well with all the students. I replied to him, "no sir, everything is fine." He sat down at the desk in front of me and looked at me, "Well, if you ever need to talk or anything, you know I'm here for you, Dustin." I thanked him, saying, "I need to be getting home, sir." He stood up and walked me to the door. No sooner had the door closed than I bolted as fast as possible toward my bike. It was the only bike left in the bike stand, and it seemed strange, as I had never had to stay back after school.

On my way to see Buck, as I approached the canal, three boys came up to me on their bikes and surrounded me. The biggest of them was the one I had knocked over on the playground. "What are you going to do now with no classroom to run to?" he challenged.

Now I'm sure I could have handled one of those boys, but not all three. They jumped off their bikes, and the big boy walked up to me and shoved me. I fell to the ground on the bike and all. The other two boys grabbed my feet and started dragging me in the dirt, and the bigger kid picked up my bike, and he was going to toss it in the canal, but just as he started to lift it up, I caught a blur of motion that passed by me. All I could do was hear the commotion… It was Buck! He knocked down the big kid and now stood in front of him and my bike with his fangs bared and his hair bristling. The other kids stopped dragging me and stood there in disbelief. As I got up from the ground and dusted myself off, I said, "You better leave me alone, or I'll sic my dog on you!" I walked over and stood next to Buck. Those two boys grabbed their bikes and sped away down the canal as fast as their feet could work the pedals.

The one kid left now stood up, never taking his eyes off Buck. "You better leave," I warned. "I ain't scared of you or your dog," he replied. At that exact moment, he took a step back and fell backward over his own bike. It was then that Buck lunged forward and bit his shoe and started yanking and growling and tossing his head left and right until the shoe came off the boy's foot. The boy struggled to get to his feet, now with only one shoe, as Buck had claimed it as his prize. "Now get out of here!" I shouted. Crying, the boy clambered on his bike and rode away as fast as possible.

I looked at Buck sitting there with the shoe in his mouth, and he seemed to be smiling at me. I sat down in the dirt, and he walked over and dropped it between my legs as if he wanted to share his prize with me. I looked at him and grabbed him by the neck, hugging him tight, and said, "It's yours, boy. Thank you, boy; I love you." I reached over and grabbed my lunch box and pulled out a Bologna sandwich, and gave it to him. We sat right there with me, holding him until the sun started to set. When I looked at Buck, he was fast asleep. I didn't want to leave, but I had to go home, or I'd get a whipping for sure. As I pedaled home, I thought about the boy and felt sorry for him. I'd never want to see anyone get hurt. When I arrived home, mother was just putting food on the table. As I walked in, Pop looked at me and said, "Holy moly, what happened to you?"

I was covered in dirt and did not know that I had ripped my shirt from the fall. Normally I would never lie, but I did not want them to know about Buck or the fight I had just been in. So I said, "I wrecked my bike down by the canal."

"Really?" said Pop, "you look like you were in a dogfight." I thought, how would he know that? Did he see the fight? I think it was just an expression, but still, it was funny to me that he'd say that because it was actually a dogfight. After dinner and some TV, it was time for bed.

Mother tucked me in, and as she left the room, she said, "Don't forget your prayers."

I climbed out of bed, got on my knees, and said my prayers. "Dear Lord, thank you for my mother and father and bless them all and my brothers too, and God, thank you for Buck, amen!" I hopped back into bed, pulled the covers up, and then added, "Oh God, please bless the little boy that he was not hurt and that he can find another shoe, amen!" and soon I was fast asleep.

Chapter Five

"Wake up, sleepy head," my mother said as she stroked my hair off my forehead while sitting on the edge of my bed, "what would you like for breakfast this morning, my pun-kin?" I looked up at her, rubbed the sleep from my eyes, and smiled. I loved it when she called me pun-kin; it was a special name that she used for me and only me.

"Pancakes and bacon," I replied.

"You got it," she said.

She stood up slowly and walked over to the window, and pulled open the curtains to let the light in, "It's going to be another beautiful day, my son." Then she turned and walked out of the room and into the kitchen. I could hear the sound of pots and pans clanking, almost like my mother was trying to sound a wake-up call for everyone in the house. I was very tired today, probably from all the excitement of the day before. I got up and went to the bathroom to wash my face, then slowly made my way to the kitchen, where I sat down at the table. I sat there with my hands propping my head up in a position from which I could watch my mother cook. Mom was a beautiful woman; she was tall with dark hair, she was always done up nice, and wore very little makeup as she was naturally beautiful.

Today she was wearing a bright yellow floral top and a pair of jeans that came down to her knees. My mother was an exceptionally good cook. Everything she made was from scratch and made with love. As she was cooking, she looked back at me and said, "So tell me, my son, who is this Buck?" She turned back to her cooking, then, still preparing our meal in silence, waiting for my reply. I could tell she was fishing for information. She must have overheard my prayers last night.

"He's a new friend, mother," I said.

"I see," she nodded. "So what about the boy who needed new shoes? Was that the same boy?" I paused for a bit to think about my answer, for I did not want to lie to my parents as I had been taught to always be honest.

I replied, "No, mother, that is a different boy; he's poor." My mother then turned to me and placed a plate of pancakes and bacon in front of me, which I started to eat. She sat down to eat with me.

She looked at me and said, "Would you like to get this friend of yours a new pair of shoes?" Thinking about it and still feeling sorry for the boy, I looked at her and smiled.

"Yes, mother, that would be nice, but I want to buy them for him."

She looked up at me and said, "That is fine, but if you don't have enough money, I will help you." "We'll go shopping later today, and maybe we can look at some other things, too," she continued. I wondered about this, and then I remembered that next Saturday was my birthday. Little did mother know, but all I wanted for my birthday was my dog Buck; well… and a shotgun, too.

Growing up, I was a little salesperson. Everyone living in town knew me. I'd pull my wagon around with cantaloupes, watermelons, newspapers, and whatever I could find, going door to door selling my products. I would also rummage through the garbage cans in the alleys around the town to collect aluminum cans and bottles which could be recycled and put money in my pocket.

Now, I had two problems at this point. One, what was the boy's shoe size, and two, how would I give the shoes to him? After all, this was the kid who wanted to smash my face. I did not have the boy's shoe with me, as I left it with Buck. It was his prize to claim, but I had to go and see if I could find it before mother and I went shopping. My brothers were just waking up. They were all in high school, and I really did not hang out with them much except for my step-brother Dell who was closer to my age.

Dell was sixteen, and I was closer to him than all my other brothers. Dell was about six feet tall, a lanky boy with brown hair, and as lazy as can be. He seemed to never leave the couch, although he would play with me whenever I asked him to. He always seemed to be watching out for me. Tony, aged seventeen, with blond hair and blue eyes, and Bryce, aged eighteen, with hair as black as night, were the two older boys, and they were pals; like spick and span, they were always together. All they were interested in were girls and cars, and sports. They all sat down for breakfast, and that was my chance to disappear for a bit. I went out the back door, hopped on my bike, and headed down the road to the thicket where Buck lived, but not before picking up a few pieces of bacon to share with him.

I walked through the thicket to the den where Buck stayed and called out to him, "Here, boy, come on, Buck!" Like an army commando, he crawled out of his den, stretched his legs out, arched his back, and sniffed the air. He knew I had something for him, as I always did.

I gave him the bacon, which he swallowed in one bite. I looked at him, asking, "Did you even taste that boy?" "I can't stay long, boy," I added and started looking for the shoe, but it was nowhere to be found. I looked at Buck and said, "Where is the shoe, boy? What did you do with it?" it occurred to me then that sometimes I would take my favorite toy to bed, so I decided that possibly, just maybe, Buck had it in his den. I laid on my belly and did the commando crawl down into his den. It was dark down there, and I could not see, and the smell of wet dog surrounded me. I felt around with my hands and grabbed a few things that felt like a shoe, and slowly made my way back to the top. When I got back into the light, I had one shoe and a raggedy old doll.

It was nice to know that Buck had some items of comfort for when he was alone. I could barely read the tag on the shoe, but I could judge it was seven and a half. I looked at Buck and said, "I love you, boy, but I've got to go." I left the shoe there for him and got home before I was even missed. Mother had just finished the morning dishes, and my brothers were all lying about on the furniture like a pack of lazy lions. Dad was out in the shop, so as my mother was getting ready, I went to the shop to see what he was doing. My dad was about five foot eleven, a big man with a beard who probably wore overalls most of his life. He was getting ready for hunting season; you see, dove season would be here in a few more days. They are very tasty little birds, and mother would take the breasts and fix them in a big pan of Spanish rice that was so delicious.

I asked my dad, "what are you doing?"

He looked at me and said, "I'm reloading some shotgun shells for hunting; you want to help?"

I said, "Yes sir, I sure do, but I do have to go with Mom to the store in a bit." Pop laid out his shells, and I inserted the primers using some kind of machine. I would pull the handle down, which would squeeze the primer into place. Next, he would add gunpowder and then a plastic wad, followed by the buckshot, and finally, I would get to pull the handle down one last time to crimp the top of the shell, and then you had a brand new shotgun shell.

I found this whole process fascinating and ingenious. After about an hour, I could hear mother calling me, "Dustin, it's time to go! Are you coming?"

I yelled back at her, "Yes, mam!"

I looked at Pop and said, "Well, I better get going, Poppa; I'll see you later." He laughed and shook his head a bit and then went back to loading the shells. Mother was already getting in the car. I looked at her and said, "Wait, I have to get some money." I ran into my room and closed the bedroom door as I did not want my brothers to see where I hid my treasures. I retrieved an old cigar box from the top shelf of the closet. I had saved over seven hundred dollars from my door-to-door sales. I did not know how much a pair of new shoes might cost, so I took out a hundred dollars and put the box back on the top shelf, and dashed outside.

As I bounced into the car, Mother said to me, "Put your seatbelt on," which I did as we headed to the store.

Chapter Six

Mother drove down Main Street. I loved to have the window down, with the cool air blowing on my face. As we passed through the town, it was fun to see all the people going about their busy days. It made me think and wonder what each one of them was doing or where they might be going.

We arrived at the shopping center, where mother parked the car, and we went inside. As soon as she entered, she met two other ladies who started talking with her and fussing over me about how cute I was. As my mother talked, I wandered to the back of the store, where shoes were displayed on a shelf. There had to be a hundred pairs of shoes there. I looked around for a bit, then an older man approached me and asked if I needed any help. His name tag said 'Buddy'. I looked up at him and said, "Yes, sir, I sure do. I'd like a seven and a half, please." He walked halfway down the aisle and stopped, and looked up at the wall.

"I have several pairs," he said to me, "do you know what color you want?"

I thought to myself the shoes the boy had were white, so I replied, "White ones, sir."

"Great! I have two on sale, one pair is twelve dollars, and one is thirty-two dollars." I looked up at Buddy, "Can you show them both to me, please?" He pulled both boxes from the shelf and had me sit down in a chair, and asked me to take my shoes off. I thought to myself, this was very strange, and said, "I'm buying these as a gift for someone else."

"I see." So he showed me the two pairs. Even the cheaper of the two pairs was better than what I was wearing, but after seeing how nice the more expensive ones were, I decided they would be a better peace offering than getting him the cheaper shoes.

He put the shoes back in the box and handed them to me. About that time, mother walked up and said to me, "Have you found what you're looking for?"

I turned to her and said, "Yes, mam."

The clerk Buddy looked up at mother and smiled, "Dolores, I have not seen you in a coon's age. How have you been?" Delighted, mother walked over and gave him a big hug. "Is this your boy?" he asked.

"Yes," mother nodded, "he's my baby," at which I blushed.

"Well, that's one polite young man you got there."

"Yes, he is, and growing up so fast," said mother. We then headed to the check-out stand, and I placed the box on the counter.

The clerk said, "That will be thirty-five dollars."

I looked at her, "The man in the back said they were thirty-two, mam."

She laughed and looked at mother, smiling, "How cute is that." Then she looked at me and said, " Well, you have to pay the governor." I thought to myself, who is this governor, and why do I have to pay him to buy some shoes? I handed her two twenties, and she gave me back a five-dollar bill. Mother and I left the store, and we walked down the sidewalk to a different store where mother had me try on some pants and some shirts, and then we got back in the car.

I looked at my mother, "I want to take you to lunch." It

was just about noon now, and we were both getting hungry. She drove down the street a bit and parked in front of her favorite Mexican restaurant. We went inside and sat down. She seemed to know the people here very well, and again they all fawned over me, "He's getting so big, he's so cute..." as I sat there blushing. Mother ordered a green chili burrito enchilada style, and I had tacos.

We ate, and the lady brought the bill and gave it to mother. "I'm paying the bill!"

I exclaimed. The waitress smiled at me, saying, "Well, ain't you the perfect gentleman." I gave her the money, then she and mother hugged, and we left.

As we drove back home, going down Main Street, we passed an old, abandoned building that used to be the car wash, and there was Buck sitting there by the side of the building. What is he doing there, I wondered. What is he up to? Just as mother drove by, I could see that on the other side of the building were two men. Both wore uniforms, and one was carrying a long pole with a rope attached to it. It was the dog catcher, but mother had turned the corner, so I was not able to see any more than that. I sat there with butterflies in my stomach and a lump in my throat. I hoped that Buck would run away so that he might not get caught. I was so worried now, but still, I could not say anything to my mother about it. '*Hurry, Mom*' was my silent thought so that we could get home,

   and then I might go help.

Chapter Seven

I could not wait to be home. I needed to go and see if Buck was okay. I think mother knew something was up because I was very quiet the rest of the way home. As we got closer to home, I said to her, "I think I'm going for a bike ride when we get home." Mother looked at me, "That is fine; just try to not stay out too late." I was out of the car and running for the bike before the car had even stopped moving. "Hold on, mister!" mother called out to me, "you'd better help me with the bags." I stopped in my tracks and hung my head down, pouting, and slowly turned around to help her. I carried the bags into the kitchen and put the box with the shoes on my bed before rushing out the door.

I vaulted onto my bike and raced toward the old car wash to see if Buck was still there. But when I arrived, there was no sign of him or the dog catchers, so I spun the bike around and headed back for the thicket where Buck lived. Arriving at his den, I called out to him, "Buck, come here, boy! Here, boy!" but he did not answer my calls. I sat down there on the ground and cried, scared of what might have happened to him. I thought, did the dog catchers get him, or maybe he was hit by a car? I did not know, and I did not like the feeling of worrying about him. I got back on my bike and started back home. I was about to cross Fourth Street, which was a busy road, and had to wait for traffic. As I was waiting for the traffic to clear, there it was, passing in front of me, the dog catchers' truck. I pedaled as fast as my little legs could go to keep up with the truck. They seemed to drive forever until they pulled into a parking lot with a white building. They drove to the back, where they started to unload the lost pets that they had caught, one by one, as I watched from a distance. First, they took out a few cats they had in smaller cages, next a black dog, then a golden retriever that looked like Mrs. Bell's dog—she was one of our neighbors—and then I got this big lump in my throat. There was Buck! They had a noose around his neck, and he was fighting them with all his might. I wanted to jump in and help him, but there was nothing I could do. They went inside the building, and the door closed behind them. I felt helpless. I climbed back on my bike and started making my way home. I cried just about all the way there. I remember how long the road appeared that day as I pedaled down our street. I didn't want to go home, but what else could I do? As I pedaled past Mrs. Bell's house, she was outside and asked me, "Have you seen Buddy?" That was the name of her dog. "He got out of the backyard today," she said. I rode up to her and told her the story of the dog catchers. She invited me in for a snack. Mrs. Bell was a very nice lady. She knew my family well. She was in her sixties, with gray hair and a warm, friendly smile. Her husband had died many years ago in the war, and she kept his medals on display with his picture over the fireplace mantel.

She looked at me and asked, "Is something troubling you, Dustin?" I confided in her about the story of my dog Buck and what we had been through. I told her every little detail, even that my parents did not know about the dog. It felt so good to share my secret with someone. She looked at me and gave me a big hug, and said, "You know he's safe right now, and it's too late to do anything about it today. I'm sure the place is closed on Sunday as well, so Monday, we will have to do something about it." She then took a warm damp cloth and wiped my face, and said, "Now don't you shed another tear about this, and run along home."

I remember as I walked inside the house, I felt a peaceful feeling come over me. She was right. Buck was safe. He might not be very happy right now, but he was safe. Mother was already fixing dinner, and pop was sitting on his chair watching the news. My dad loved his news. I think it was probably his favorite program on TV. I climbed up in his lap and put my arms around his neck. "Boy, did you have a bad day today?" he asked me.

"No, it wasn't too bad, Poppa." He looked at me and smiled, "How about Sunday we take a drive and go, scout? Where are we going to go dove hunting?"

My eyes lit up with excitement, "Heck yes, I wanna go!" He laughed at my excitement, and we sat there together, watching the news until I fell asleep in his arms.

At dinner time, mother called out, though it did not take much for me to wake up as I was starving. Pop looked at me and said, "Boy, you were out like a light, or did my news put you to sleep?" My brothers were home and sitting at the table with our mother. They all seemed to be waiting for me and pop. It was my turn to say grace, so I sat down at the table, reached out, and grabbed my mother's hand. My brothers looked at me in a funny way as we had never prayed like this before. My mother took father's hand, and father took Dell's until we all formed a chain around the table. Once connected, I bowed my head and said, "Dear Lord, thank you for all that you have given us. Thank you for my wonderful family. Please bless this food that it will nourish our bodies, and dear Lord, a special blessing to Mrs. Bell that she will find her dog, Buddy. Thanks again for these things we pray for. Amen!"

It was a quiet dinner after that until father spoke and said, "We will have to pray that way at every meal. Mister, where did you pick that up from?"

I looked at him and said, "I don't know; I just felt like doing it."

"Well, it was a good thing, boy," father said to me. I did not know this at the time, but now holding hands while praying has become our family tradition and will always be. After dinner was done, I helped my mother with the dishes. We sat in the living room and watched some TV, and then it was off to bed.

Mother came in and tucked me in and kissed me on my forehead, and said, "I'm very proud of you, my little man." She stroked my hair. I closed my eyes and was fast asleep.

Chapter Eight

Sunday morning, I awoke to my mother singing in the kitchen and the smell of bacon and eggs cooking. Mother asked if I was going to church with her. I looked over at Papa, and he said, 'I think he's going with me to scout for some good hunting places today." I was ready to leave right after breakfast. I was all dressed up in my floppy Boone hat, camouflage pants, and shirt. Papa looked at me and laughed, and said, "Boy, we're not going hunting today; we're only scouting for a place to hunt."

"I know," I said, "It's just that I don't want the birds to see me scouting."

"Good point," he replied, grabbing his camouflage hat and coat. We jumped in the Jeep and were about ready to drive off when mother came out and handed us a couple of sack lunches. She told us to be safe, kissed Papa on the cheek, and then we were off. We drove out into the desert quite a ways until we were pretty close to the Colorado River, knowing that since it was the desert, the birds would be coming there for water, so it was a great place to set up for hunting. The smell of rain was in the air, and it was an overcast day. I honestly think dad just wanted to go out for a drive. We drove the Jeep up this long road till we were on top of the mountain. When the road came to an end, we walked up the hill a little more until we got to the top, from where you could see for miles, and it felt like you were on top of the world. We sat down on a big flat rock and started to eat the lunch our mother had made for us. As we ate, I looked up at Pop and said, "Why don't we have a dog? I mean, the dog would be great for hunting..."

He looked at me and nodded, and said, "Sure would." I smiled back at him and said we should get one then. Not another word was said about it. I guess I was just planting the seed. We finished our lunch and walked back to the Jeep. We drove around some more. On the way, we spotted a family of desert burros, but they were gone just as soon as we spotted them. My dad called them ghosts of the desert for just that reason. We arrived home around sunset. Mother was just setting the table when we walked in. "Are you boys hungry?" she asked.

I replied, "I'm so hungry I could eat a horse."

I asked Mother how she liked church and what the lesson was today. She said it was about forgiveness. The preacher talked about asking for forgiveness for all that you have done wrong or for those whom you have hurt in any way and about having a clean slate, which will grant you your room in the heavenly father's house. We finished off the night by playing cards and just being together as a family until it was time for us to go to bed. On my way to my room, I asked my mother if we had some wrapping paper, so she came in and sat on the edge of my bed and helped me wrap up the shoes for the boy from school. "When are you going to give them to him?" she asked.

"I think I will when we go to lunch tomorrow," I told her. "I just want to do it in private because I don't want him to be embarrassed or anything like that."

"That's very sweet of you," mother said as she finished helping me wrap the present. She then tucked me in for the night. Mother looked at me and said goodnight sleep tight, don't let the bedbugs bite, then she kissed me on the forehead and left the room.

I closed my eyes and prayed again, "Dear lord, thank you for the great day with my dad. Please bless my family and keep us all safe. God, please help Buck to get out of the pound. I want him to come and live with me, God. I hope you can make this happen. Amen." I closed my eyes, and when I woke up the next morning, it was late. It was a Monday, and I had to get to school. I picked up my lunch and put the present into my backpack, and pedaled my way to school. Mrs. Bell, our neighbor, was out front watering her yard. I stopped for just a moment to say, "Hi, are you going to get your dog Buddy today?"

She looked at me and replied, "Yes, about noon."

I looked at her and told her, "Please say hi to Buck for me."

She said, "I sure will, Dustin. Now you get along before it's too late."

I could not wait for the day to be over. I wanted to go and check at the dog pound. I was anxious all day and just wanted it to be over. Lunchtime came. I sat in my usual spot by the baseball backstop and started to eat my lunch. Off in the distance on the other side of the playground, I could see the boy I had gotten into a fight with. I lifted my backpack and my lunch sack and headed over to see him. As I walked up to him, he did not say a word. His clothes were tattered, most likely hand-me-downs from his older brother like mine. I sat down in front of him and pulled out my lunchbox. "You want a sandwich?" I asked. He gazed at me without saying a word and turned his head away. "I'm Dustin, by the way," I continued. "I wanted to tell you that I was sorry about my dog and wanted to make it up to you." He glanced at me, then again looked away.

Presently he said, "How would you do that?"

"Well," I said, "first, I want to ask for your forgiveness, and then I want to give you something." I reached into my backpack and pulled out his gift, laying the box on the ground in front of him. He looked at it but did not touch it. I could tell he felt awkward about the whole thing. I stood up and said to him, "You know I really just want to be your friend." I pulled out a sandwich from my lunch sack and set it on top of the gift before turning and walking away. A few minutes later, the bell rang, and all the kids returned to their classrooms. I couldn't wait for school to be over that day.

Chapter Nine

The three o'clock bell rang, and Mr. Deter was handing out homework assignments to each of the students as we walked out the door. As I approached him, he looked at me and said, "I want you to write a story on friendship. You have until Friday to turn it in." I smiled at him and headed toward my bike. All this took a while, and most of the kids had already left. I was bent down, unchaining my bike, when I heard a voice, soft and low, saying, "My name's Christian." I looked up, and it was that boy.

I extended my hand to him, "Christian, my name is Dustin." We shook hands. I asked him, "Do you want to ride home with me?"

"Sure," he nodded. I looked down, and on his feet were the new shoes I had given to him. He seemed happier. We swung up on our bikes and took off. He was bigger than me, so he was much faster than me on his bike, although I did my best to keep up with him.

We stopped for a minute at a corner, and I said to him, "I want to show you something." He followed me over to the old canal, where we laid our bikes down, and I took him through the thicket.

"Where are we going?" Christian asked.

"You'll see," I answered, somewhat mysteriously. We came upon the den where Buck lived, and we both sat down. I looked at him and said, "My dog Buck lives here," but he seemed incredulous.

I confided in him as I had with Mrs. Bell and told him the whole story. He laughed at the part about me digging out his old shoe from Buck's den. We sat there and chucked rocks and poked things with sticks and talked for about an hour, then left, and he followed me home. I wanted him to meet my mother, so we parked our bikes in the front yard and walked inside. Mother was in the kitchen fixing dinner as we walked in, and I said to her, "Mother, this is Christian."

She looked at him and said, "Nice to meet you, Christian. Would you like to stay for dinner?"

Christian replied, "No, mam I can't. My dad is waiting, and I have to go, but thanks."

"Okay," mother said, "but you're going to miss out on some good cooking." We laughed.

Christian looked at me and said, "I gotta get going, or I'm going to get a whooping." I walked outside with him. He picked up his bike, saying, "My friends call me Chris, so you can call me that, okay?"

I smiled as wide as possible and said, "I'll see you tomorrow, Chris," and he pedaled away. As he reached the end of the block, he turned around and waved goodbye to me.

I walked over to Mrs. Bell's house and knocked on the door. She opened the door, saying to me, "About time you came over."

I walked in and looked up at her, and asked, "Did you get Buddy out of jail?"

She smiled at me, "Of course I did! And thanks for letting me know where he was, too."

"Did you see Buck?"

"Oh yes, he was doing fine," she nodded, "in fact, he and

Buddy were cellmates." That made me laugh. She looked at me and gave me a big hug. "I got something I want to show you," she stood up and went to her back door and opened it up. Buddy came in, wagging his tail, just as happy as could be. He came up to me and started licking my face as if to say thank you. I looked up, and Buck was standing in the doorway, tail wagging.

I fell to my knees and said, "Buck, my boy!" with my arms stretched out, and he ran to me so hard and fast he knocked me over and laid right on top of me as if unwilling to let me go and he licked my face no end. Although I was so happy I started crying, because I had feared that he was gone from my life forever.

"Mrs. Bell, how did this happen?" I wondered.

She said, "Well, when I went to the dog pound to get Buddy, I walked in and was able to watch the two of them playing together. I knew that Buddy needed a friend to play with… he doesn't get enough exercise from an old lady like me, so I adopted Buck for you." She handed me a paper; it was an adoption paper, and under the owner's name, it had Mrs. Bell and my name right beside hers.

I got up off the floor with tears streaming down my face and wrapped my arms around her, and hugged her as tightly as possible, "Thank you, thank you, thank you!"

She hugged me back, then sat down at the table and looked me right in my eyes, and said, "Now, there are some responsibilities that you will have to take." She continued as I wiped the tears from my face, "You will need to take both dogs for walks and help clean up the mess in my backyard, and on weekends you can come over and feed the dogs too."

I put my hand out and said, "Deal!" She shook it and pulled me close, and gave me another hug.

I went over to Buck and held him tight around his neck, saying, "I got to go, boy; you stay here and be good. I love you." I left and went back home.

When I walked in the door, my older brother Dell said to me, "Was that Chris Hanson you were with today?"

I looked at him and shrugged, "Well, I don't know his last name, but yes, his name was Chris."

"I know his older brother," said Dell, "and that family is bad news."

I thought about Chris and how that day, he was sitting alone in the playground. I remembered his clothes being worn and slightly tattered; he had seemed very sad as if he did not have a friend in the world.

Maybe his family was not very nice to him. Well, he was my friend now, and that was all that mattered. Overhearing, mother said, "Why don't you invite Chris to your birthday party this weekend?"

I looked up at her and said, "Thanks, Mom."

Dinner time came, and we all linked hands around the table. Mother decided to bless the food this evening. I got goosebumps when my mother asked God to bless Chris and his family. I squeezed her hand tight during the prayer as if to say a quiet thank you. After dinner, we all watched Pop's favorite show on TV, and I fell asleep on the couch as I normally did. The joke around the house was that as soon as the sun went down, my eyes closed, and that is pretty much the truth even to this day.

I was awakened by my older brother Bryce nudging me with his foot to get up and go to bed. His foot was in my face, almost touching my nose, so I reached out and bit him hard right on the toe. As he fell back screaming in agony, I got up and ran to my room and locked the door, with Bryce pounding on my door, "I'm going to get you, you little brat!"

Father came out, demanding, "What's all this commotion about?" "

That little brat bit my toe," Bryce explained.

"Now, how could that have happened?" my father asked.

I yelled through the door, "Because he stuck it in my face

when I was sleeping!"

"Well, you're lucky then, Bryce, because I would have bit it plumb off if it were me! Now you go to bed!"

I kept my door locked all night, just in case. Bryce was my older brother, but he was not a friend. He was always mean to me; I guess it made him feel like a strong guy to pick on someone younger. My stepbrother Dell was always the one to stand up for me and protect me as a brother should, and I looked up to him in so many ways. I finally settled down and said my prayers, and fell asleep, dreaming of adventures of a new day.

Chapter Ten

I woke up early today to get ready for school, even before my mother or father. By the time they got up, I was already fixing them breakfast. Pop walked into the kitchen, asking, "What are you doing, boy?" I looked at him, "Fixing everyone's breakfast… oatmeal and toast, and the coffee are all ready for you." "Wow!" he exclaimed, "Aren't you the early bird, and how did you know oatmeal was exactly what I was going to fix this morning?" I laughed because I knew he was being sarcastic. When mother walked in, she was quite pleased, you know how nice it is to have someone else cook for you for a change. I looked up at her and smiled my biggest smile. The oatmeal came out perfect, though the toast was slightly burnt, but that's the way poppa liked it.

Soon my brothers were all awake and moving about the house. Bryce walked by me and, when no one was looking, slapped me on the back of my head, which made me drop the toast on the floor, which I picked up without saying a word while he laughed at me. I set it aside and made some more. Dell and Tony sat at the table, waiting for their food. I dished them up some oatmeal and two pieces of buttery toast. Tony, who was two years older than I was, was slightly plump with red hair and thrived on skateboards and video games. He was not much of a socializer except during breakfast. Tony looked at me and said, "Thanks for the awesome food, bro," trying to fit in with his jar-gin.

I said, "No, problem, dude." I had to laugh in my head about it.

Bryce came to the table and sat down, saying, "Dish it up, slave!" So I filled a big bowl with yummy oatmeal and set it down in front of him. "Where's my toast?" he demanded.

"Oh," I said, "let me get it." I walked over and picked up the toast he had made me drop on the floor and put it in front of him, saying, "Here is the toast I made for you." He grabbed a piece and started munching it down.

As he ate it, I added, "Next time, try not to make me drop it on the dirty floor…" and I walked out of the room to the sound of Tony and Dell laughing.

I finished up breakfast and headed out for school. On the way stopping at Mrs. Bell's to help out and see Buck. I knocked on the door. "Come on in," she said; the doors opened, and she was sitting at the kitchen table having tea and reading the newspapers. "Isn't it your birthday this weekend?"

I looked at her and smiled, and replied, "Yes, mam, I'll be thirteen." "You are growing up way too fast, mister! The dogs are in the backyard along with the poop scoop."

"Okay," I nodded as I made my way to the back door. I opened the door slowly so as to not let the dogs inside the house. Buddy and Buck must be best of friends by now. I thought as I closed the door. Behind me, the two dogs were cuddled up in a dog pile. I walked up and nestled right in with them both. Buck started licking my face and wagging his tail. I said, "I miss you, boy… wish you could stay with me." He thumped his tail even harder on the ground in excitement. I gave them both a big hug and said, "I have to get to work." I grabbed the poop scoop and started the cleanup. Not the most glamorous of jobs but an important one, I thought as I cleaned up the yard. "You dogs poop way too much," and I laughed.

I finished my chores and then put my arms around Buck and hugged him hard and long. "I've got to get going, boy. School day, ya know." I went back inside, put my arms around Mrs. Bell, and said, "I'll be back to take them for a walk after school."

She smiled at me and said, "Well, be here." I walked outside and got astride my bike.

Buck was there at the front fence to see me off. I looked at him and called out, "Don't worry, boy, I'll be back."

It was a long day at school. Rain was in the air; you could

smell it. Here in the desert, we only get rain a few times a year. Some people hated it, but not me, because it was such a rare thing. I loved it, it would pour, and I would be playing in the rain, drenched from head to toe—well, at least until a big crack of thunder would roll across the sky, then I'd run back into the house like a scared little kitten.

During recess, it started drizzling. I looked all over the playground for Chris, but he was nowhere to be found in the school that day. I thought to myself that I would stop by his house on the way home. Then the recess bell rang, and I headed back to class. I sat and listened to the lesson, but at the same time was daydreaming of playing with Buck after school. Mr. Deter called on me, "So Dustin, how's your story going?" I was startled, as I had been daydreaming and was not paying attention.

"Um… it's going good," I replied.

"Can you read a bit to us?" he raised an eyebrow.

"Yea," I stuttered, then snatched up my notepad and began to read. All of a sudden, there was a terrible clap of thunder, and the lights went out. There were only twenty minutes left in the school day, so Mr. Deter let everyone go home early. Saved by a thunderstorm!

I ran to the bike rack, unlocked my bike, and headed toward Chris's house. As I rolled into the driveway, I noticed that the house was run down, with paint peeling off the walls. There were a few old broken-down cars in the yard and garbage all over. I knocked on the door, and a sandy blond boy answered.

"We're not buying anything," he said as soon as he swung the door open.

I stammered, "Is…is Chris there?"

The door closed, and I heard him yell, "Chris! One of your little friends is at the door!"

The door opened a crack. It was Chris peeking outside, "What's up?" he asked.

I replied, "I did not see you at school today and wanted to make sure you were okay. Are you ill?"

Chris said, "I can't talk right now."

"Okay," as I turned to walk away,

I paused and said, "Oh, I almost forgot… you're invited to my birthday party this Saturday. Don't worry about a present either."

He said, "Okay!" and shut the door.

On my way home, I thought it was strange that Chris did not open the door all the way or at least come outside. Maybe he was embarrassed about his home; I was not sure, but something did not feel right.

Chapter Eleven

Morning arrived, and the house was quiet as we all got up to get ready for school. On the table was a plate of toast and freshly cut fruit that mother had set out for us boys. Lunch bags were lined up on the countertop, with our names on each bag. I ate breakfast, snatched up my lunch, and walked my bike over to Mrs. Bell's house. She was already at the door, waiting for me. "Right on time!" she said to me. I went inside and sat at the table with her. "Would you like some tea?" she asked me.

I replied, "No, not this morning, but thanks so much." She smiled warmly at me and took a sip from her cup.

Nothing like some good tea to warm you up in the morning. I smiled back at her. "Well, I'm going to get to work," I said.

I excused myself from the table and went out back, where both dogs were waiting for me wagging their tails. Buck had a ball in his mouth, which I had to wrestle from him so I could toss it for him. He would prance around the yard to retrieve it; it was comical to watch him and Buddy play chase with each other.

I cleaned up the yard and sat on the back porch with the dogs. Buck would stare at me with his brown eyes as if he wanted something. I asked him, "What ya want, boy?" He'd turn his head slightly to the left as cute as can be. I reached into my lunch bag and pulled out a sandwich that my mother had made for me. "Remember these, boy?" It had been quite some time since he had a sandwich. I tore it in half and gave each of them a half, saying, "Okay, I gotta get going to school, guys." I grabbed Buck by the neck and gave him a long, tight hug.

Mrs. Bell standing behind the screen door, said, "You love that dog a lot, don't you, son?"

I looked up at her as she smiled at me, "Yes, mam, with all my heart."

As I entered the house, she reached out and messed my hair, and I proceeded to leave. "Thanks again; see you later today."

"Okay, mam," I said, then climbed on my bike and pushed off to school.

At lunchtime, Chris was sitting at the edge of the playground, all alone. As I approached him, he turned to me and snapped, "Go away!"

"Why?" I asked.

"Just go away," he said again.

I walked around in front of him and sat down. "Chris, what's wrong? I wanted to share my lunch with you." He sat quietly while I lifted a pudding cup and placed it on the ground in front of him.

He reached out and picked it up, pulled the lid off, and started eating it. "Thanks," he said. I moved closer to him to find out what was wrong. Gazing at him,

I said, "You know you are my best friend, Chris, and you can tell me anything, okay?" He finished off the pudding and set the cup down, raised his head, then reached back and slowly pulled his hoodie back off of his face and head. "Wow!" I exclaimed, "What happened to you?" Chris was sporting a nice shiner with a cut upper lip, but he said nothing happened and quickly pulled the hoodie back into place. "Did one of your brothers beat you up? Did you get into a fight? Did you fall down?

What happened to you? Tell me!" I insisted.

He looked up at me with a tear rolling down his cheek, "It was my dad who did this." I did not know what to say; I only thought about how I would feel if my dad had done this to me. I still did not understand at this time what Chris was going through at home.

I asked, "Why, why would he do that to you, Chris?"

He looked awkwardly at me and said, "He had a bad day, I guess, and was upset. He saw my new shoes, and he wanted to know where I got them. When I told him, he hit me with the back of his hand. Don't you ever lose a fight again, boy! I'll make a man of you yet." I was so scared; I didn't know what to do.

The bell rang, so we all returned to class. While walking with Chris, I said to him, "I'm sorry about all of this. You know I will talk to your dad if you like."

"No," he shook his head, "You'll just make things worse."

"Okay," I nodded, "oh, by the way… my mom said you can come over for dinner tonight if you wish."

Chris looked at me and said, "Yes, that would be nice."

"Great!" I nodded. "About five o'clock then, okay?"

The day went by pretty fast, well at least it seemed that way, and then finally, the three o'clock bell rang. "Don't forget that your report needs to be completed and turned in tomorrow," Mr. Deter said as we walked out the door. I was almost finished with mine; just another hour or so, and it would be ready to turn in. I met Chris at the bike rack to ride home with him. As we pedaled away together, he asked me how my dog was doing. He also told me he had a dog once, but he ran off because Chris' dad was mean to him, and one day the dog just disappeared. I arrived at Chris's house and talked for a bit on his front porch when a truck pulled up in the driveway. Chris glanced quickly at me, "It's my dad. You had better leave."

But as I was putting on my bike helmet, Chris' dad got out of the truck and walked up to Chris and me, and asked, "Who is this kid?"

Chris looked up at him, "This is Dustin from school. He's my friend."

His dad glared at me and said, "Ain't this the boy that sicked his dog on ya?" I started walking towards my bike. "Boy, I'm talking to ya," he said in a gruff, low voice.

I turned around and looked at him and said, "Sir, it was not like that; my dog was just protecting me."

He walked up to me and grabbed me by the arm tightly,

and pulled me close to him; then he got down on one knee and looked me right in my eyes, leaned over, and whispered in my ear, "If I ever see that dog of yours I'll make sure you will never see him again boy, and I don't ever want to see you again either!" Then he released me and turned and walked into his house, yelling to Chris, "Get in the house, boy, playtime is over!" I had never been so scared in my life. My eyes watered up as I rode home, but first, I stopped at Mrs. Bell's house to take care of the dogs.

She was sitting in a chair on the front porch as I rode up. "They're waiting for you," she laughed. I walked into the back, and as she had told me, they were both sitting watching the back door, as if I was expected. I did my chores and played with them both for a bit, then called Buck to me.

He walked up to me, knowing I was feeling bad. I hugged him tight around his neck. "I will never let anything happen to you, boy," I said as I wept, and he licked my tears away. I finished up and headed home. When I walked in the door, the house was quiet, so I went to my room and finished my homework to turn in the next day.

Right before dinner time, my mother asked me, "Did you invite your friend over?"

I said, "Yes, mam, he said he would be here, and I told him five o'clock." But Chris never showed up that night at all.

Chapter Twelve

I was very worried about Chris after what his dad said to me and that he did not show up for dinner as we had planned. The next day at school, I waited at the bike rack for him to arrive. When he pulled up, and I greeted him, asking, "What happened to you last night? I thought you were coming over for dinner?" he was quiet and did not say a word to me. I could tell something was very wrong with him. He parked his bike and started walking to his class, looking at the ground and walking away from me. He would not look at me or talk to me in any way. "Chris!" I said loudly, "what's wrong?" He said nothing; he just kept walking away from me. I did not know what to do, so I yelled at him, "See you at lunch!" before he disappeared around the corner of the building.

I slowly made my way to class, thinking to myself, what could I have done? How come he won't talk to me? It wasn't until lunchtime when things became a lot clearer to me. As the lunch bell rang, I took my lunch sack and hurried to the playground. There was Chris at the far end of the playground where he usually sat. I walked up and sat down next to him. "My mom made you lunch today, too," and I handed him his sandwich.

He looked up at me and said, "My dad said we can't be friends and that I can't see you anymore."

I looked at Chris and asked, "Why, Chris, what did I do? You're my best friend."

"He's mad at me," was his reply, "He said I'm a lousy son, and he wished I was never born."

I could see the tears in his eyes, so I reached out and put one hand on his shoulder, saying, "It's okay, Chris. It does not matter what he said. You're still my friend." He pulled away in pain when I touched him. "What's wrong, are you hurt?" I was alarmed. Tears were streaming down his cheek as he lifted up his shirt, and I could see the bruises and the welts from the belt across his back and stomach. It made me sick to even look at such a sight, and I thought to myself, how can a father do this to his child? There was no love in that house at all, the love that a child needs and the warmth that a son needs from his father.

Chris looked up at me and said, "Promise me that you will not tell anyone."

I crossed my fingers behind my back and said, "I promise." We finished our lunch, and the bell rang, and we trooped back into class.

I could not concentrate at all while in class. All I could think about was my friend Chris. How can I help him? What can I do, I asked myself over and over again, but each time coming up with the same answer— there was nothing I could do except tell an adult—the teacher, my mom, or dad. But if I did that, I would certainly lose my friend's trust. Then it came to me, Mrs. Bell! I would talk to her after school... I knew I could trust her.

School bell rang, and three o'clock could not have come sooner. I sprinted to the bike rack and met Chris as usual, and we rode home together. About a block from his house, we parted ways for fear that his dad might see us together.

I went directly over to Mrs. Bell's house. She opened the door and said, "Looks like you have had a rough day."

I said, "Yes, mam, it was not my best." I gathered the

leashes and rounded up the dogs for their walk. We took off and went a few blocks to the city park, where I would spend the next hour tossing the ball over and over for Buck and Buddy. Buck would grab the ball and want Buddy to chase him. It was such a sight to see these two, once strangers now best friends, kind of like Chris and me. As I sat in the grass, Buck would come over to me and lie down beside me with his head on my leg as if to console me. I scratched his head and said to him, how can a father beat his son like that, so brutally.

If my dad ever hit me like that, I'd run away from home for sure. When I arrived back at Mrs. Bell's house, she was in the kitchen baking some fresh banana bread, and the aroma filled the house. "Smells good, mam," I said.

"Thank you," she replied, "well, put the dogs out back and come back in and have a slice with some milk," which I did. I sat at her table as she sliced off a piece and set it down in front of me. When she sat down and asked, "Why so troubled, son?" I looked up at her with tears in my eyes and told her my story. She was astonished and sorrowful about Chris. I asked her not to tell anyone, but what she said to me made a lot of sense. "What if you said nothing, and the next beating took Chris's life? You would lose your friend forever. Now, what if you told someone and they were able to do something to help Chris? Maybe he will be mad at you and not want to be your friend anymore."

"That would be bad, too," I said.

Mrs. Bell replied, "Yes, but in both situations, though you might lose your friend, but at least you would save his life, to hopefully be his friend again someday." When I finished eating, Mrs. Bell gave me a big hug goodbye, and then I walked home.

That night at home, I thought a lot about what Mrs. Bell had said. After dinner, I helped mother do the dishes, and I told her that I would like to talk to her and father. They both came in and sat down at the kitchen table. "What seems to be troubling you, buckaroo?" my father asked. "It's my friend Chris…" I told them about Chris and his father and how that man was beating Chris so badly. I looked at my mother and said he might not be alive if we just did nothing. I also told them how his father grabbed me and made threats. I could see pop getting angry about my story; he was not angry at me but at what I was saying. We finished the night with a movie and some yummy strawberry shortcake mother had made for us.

As I lay in bed, Mother came in and sat down beside me and held my hand, "Oh, my little man!" she said, "You're growing up way too fast, but I'm so proud of you for bringing this to us."

"I just want Chris to be safe," I said.

"He will be," mother said, "we just need to keep him in our prayers, and the good Lord will watch over him."

One more day of school and the weekend would be here. I was excited about having a birthday party; it meant getting cake and ice cream and playing games, and, most of all, the presents. The next morning at about two A.M., I was awakened by the sound from next door. It was Buck; he was howling as if he was calling me. Silently I walked to the slider door off the kitchen and opened it up just enough for me to squeeze out. I then walked over to the fence and climbed on top of an old barrel my father had been storing, "Buck!" I whispered. He jumped on the fence, standing and stretching out to touch me. I was able to reach my hand over the fence just enough to rub him on his nose and ears. "Boy, what's wrong," I asked, "you miss me, don't you?" I stayed out with him for about a half hour, and then he licked my hand. "Boy, I've got to be going to bed. If I get caught out here, I will get a whopping for sure." I turned and proceeded back to the house, walked inside, and slowly closed the sliding door behind me. I woke up the next morning tired from last night; even my mother said to me that I looked tired, so I must have been. She packed our lunches and waved us all goodbye as we headed off to school.

I waited at the bike rack for Chris. He showed up just in time as the bell rang, and as he approached, I could tell something was not right. He was hurting again. "Are you okay, Chris?" I asked.

He looked at me and said, "No, my ribs are hurting." "Was it your father again? He beat you again..."

Chris started walking to his class, but as he passed me, he said to me, "I'm going to run away tonight."

"No, Chris, don't do that," I said. "Please just come to my house after school, and you can stay with me, okay?"

"I don't know. I think my dad might find me there and hurt me some more."

I put my arm around his shoulder and said, "Chris, I promise you will be safe at my house. My mom and pop will not let anything happen to you at all." The day seemed to drag on. When the lunchtime bell sounded, I hurried to the place where Chris and I always met and had lunch, but Chris was not there, so I made my way to the office and asked them if anyone had seen Chris.

The nice lady at the front counter said, "Oh yes, his father came and picked him up from school today as he was not feeling good." My heart almost stopped when she told me this. All I could think of the rest of the day was, what if Chris was hurt or dead? What then? As soon as the bell jangled at the end of the day, I ran as fast as I could to the bike rack. Chris's bike was still there, so I rode my bike and held the handlebars of his all the way to my house. As I approached the house, I could see father out in the driveway working on his truck.

"Whose bike is that?" he asked. I dropped them both and ran to him, and put both my arms around him with tears rolling down my face. I told him what had happened. "Put the bike in the back of the truck," he said to me in a very stern voice. "We will take the bike back to his house together, okay?" I hopped in the cab after putting Chris's bike in the back of the truck. Father drove all the way there without talking at all. As we pulled into the driveway, father looked at me and said, "You stay in this truck, boy, and don't get out for anything."

"Yes, sir," I replied. Father started walking toward the front door. When it opened, Chris's father stepped out.

"What do you want?" he asked my father.

"Well, we brought Chris his bike back. He left it at school; is he here?"

"Chris!" his father yelled, "this man's got your bike." Chris poked his head out of the door. "Get along, boy, go get it out of the man's truck. Chris walked close to the truck, and I could see he had a black eye now and was still walking in pain.

As Chris approached my father, pop got down on one knee, "Come here, boy," he said. Chris walked up to my dad. When he lifted up his shirt, I was almost sickened by the black and blue marks and bruises on his body. "Get in the truck," father said to him as he stood up. Chris climbed up in the cab with me. As father turned to look at me, I could see the rage in his eyes. Then he turned and started walking towards Chris's father.

"What the heck you think you're doing, boy?" Chris's father hollered.

"He's doing as I asked," Pop said as he stepped even closer to Chris's father. "So you think it's okay to beat up little kids, do ya? You're a big man, aren't you? If you ever lay a hand on my son again, it will be your last." At this time, they both were face to face.

Chris's father said, "Well, it's my boy, and I can do what I like to him if he doesn't listen." He shoved my father back with both hands, and as he did, my father tripped on something in the yard and fell back. But pop was up and on his feet in a heartbeat. This time he charged forward and tackled Chris's dad on the front porch and proceeded to beat the heck out of Chris's dad.

When father stood up, he looked down at Chris's dad and said, "You will never touch either one of these boys again, you hear, or I will be back and give you some more of this!" he said, "You don't beat a child like that!" He turned and walked away while Chris's father was still lying on the porch. Father got in the truck and looked at Chris, and said, "Chris, you are going to stay with us for now until your father is better, okay?"

"Thank you, sir," Chris murmured.

When we got back home, Mother and Dell were setting the table. "That smells good," Pop said as we walked through the door. Mother had roasted a small turkey with all the trimmings; it was like an early Thanksgiving.

"I see you brought your friend home for dinner," Mother said. "I will set another place at the table." I could see Chris smile in delight.

Dell walked up to Chris and introduced himself, "I'm Dell," he said, and he stuck out his hand, "and the two lazy ones on the couch are Tony and Bryce."

Tony looked up and said, "Hi!" Bryce did not even act like anyone was there.

Mother said, "Well, I hope you're hungry, boys. Dinner

will be in like half an hour." Mother and father disappeared into their bedroom; I assumed to discuss the prior events. Chris and I went into my room so I could get him lined out with sleeping arrangements and all.

Chis and I sat on the bed, and I looked at him eye to eye and said, "Chris, I'm sorry about your pop, man, but you know he can't just keep on hitting you like this."

"I know," Chris replied. I could see the tears starting to well up in his eyes, and then a single tear ran down his face.

"Hey!" I said, "it's okay now… you're with friends that care about you." I reached out and put my hand on his shoulder, "you're my best friend, and I don't want to see you hurt anymore. It will get better; we have to just give it some time, okay?"

He looked at me and smiled, "I love my dad. Even though he's mean to me and hits me, he's my father, and I love him."

"I know," I replied to Chris, "but your father has got to show you that same love back. Maybe we can get him some help or something. My mom and pop will figure it out; I promise you that."

We all sat down to a great dinner. Mother reached out and took Chris's hand, saying, "Dustin, will you say the blessing tonight?"

As we all held hands, I started to pray, "Dear Lord, Bless this food, that it will give us strength and nourishment, bless this family in health and happiness, dear Lord."

We also asked for a special blessing for my friend Chris and his family, that love would find their home and that Chris's father would not be sick anymore. "Please help his family, God! Thank you so much for all that you have given us, and thank you so much for giving Chris to me as a friend and please bless Buck and Mrs. Bells. We pray for these things in God's name, amen!" We ate like kings that night. Bellies full, me and Chris helped mother with the dishes, and we all sat at the table and played some cards before bedtime. It was a good night full of joy and happiness.

"Off to bed!" Pop said.

Mother came in to tuck us in, "You boys get to sleep now; we have a big day tomorrow." She leaned over and kissed Chris and me right on the forehead, and left the room. "Good night, my two angels," she said as she closed the bedroom door.

Chapter Thirteen

Saturday morning, I was awake with the birds, as I knew this was my day. I was so excited I could not lay in bed for another second. I ran down the hall into the living room to see that I was the only one awake! It was only 5 a.m. when I looked at the clock. I had better be quiet, I said to myself, and went back to my room to get dressed. Chris was sound asleep. I could not help but think about what was going on in his head as he lay there asleep, but at the same time, I felt better knowing that he was safe. I scooped up my coat and wriggled through the slider out toward the backyard fence to see Buck. I climbed over the fence. This time, Buck and Buddy were both standing there wagging their tails as if they were waiting for me. Buck came up to me as I got down on my knees, so happy to see me and licking my face. "I love you, boy," I said and hugged his neck. "I miss you so much. I wish you could come to stay with me forever," I said to him. Then he lay down on the ground, so I laid next to him right there on the grass, and the next thing I knew, I was fast asleep with my arm around him.

I woke to the sound of Mrs. Bell laughing. "Now that's a sight to see! How did you get back here?"

"I climbed the fence," I said to her. "Well, get up and help me feed these two hungry boys," she said, which I did. Once I had finished, she invited me in for some cocoa.

"I can only stay a bit as my mom 'n pop don't know where I am."

"Okay," she replied, "oh, and happy birthday," she said to me.

"Thank you," I grinned with a hot cocoa mustache on my face. Having downed the cocoa, I said, "Well, I need to be getting back before I'm missed…thanks again, Mrs. Bell." I gave her a big hug, and she messed up my hair as I headed out the front door. When I got back home, Dell and Tony were in the front room watching TV.

Tony looked at me, "Where the heck were you, kiddo?"

I explained that I needed to help Mrs. Bell with some chores. "Wow!" he said, "are you trying to earn a merit badge?" They both started to laugh a bit. I even thought it was kind of funny myself. Going into my room, I climbed back into bed, and as I did so, Chris started to wake up.

"Good morning!" he said to me.

"Yes, it is!" I exclaimed. "It's going to be a beautiful sunny day." Chris rolled over so that we were face to face.

"Man," he said, "I can't believe what happened yesterday between your dad and mine.. still seems like I'm dreaming."

"Yes, I know," I agreed, "I have never seen my pop that upset, but at the same time, I'm sure he was not happy about his actions."

That very moment we heard my dad's voice calling, "Dustin, Chris! You boys get in here!" We both got up, and Pop was standing at the end of the hall with his bedroom door open, "Come on in here, you two. I want to talk to you both." "Chris." he said, "I want to tell you I'm sorry. What I did yesterday was wrong; I let my anger get the better of me, but at the same time, what your father is doing to you is wrong, too, and it's criminal to beat a child like that. No child should be treated in that manner. I want to ask you both to forgive me for this, boys, and I want you both to pray about it and pray for Chris's father that he may heal inside. I don't know for the life of me why he is so troubled inside, but we need to bring this to God and put it in his hands. Okay, boys, do you understand what I mean?" We both nodded, and Chris put his hand out to shake my dad's hand and said thanks to him.

"My father has had some terribly bad times since my mother passed away last year. He used to be a father just like you are, and we used to play catch and hang out together, but after my mom died, all that seemed to change. He spends a lot of time alone, and he drinks a lot too. I know he needs some help."

Father nodded and said, "Well, that's between God and his son; he has got to want to change."

Chris and I got dressed for the day and went for a short bike ride. We stopped at Wilson's Creek Park to rest, and as we sat on the swing set resting, Chris said wistfully, "Happy Birthday! I wish I had a gift for you, Dustin."

I looked at him as I stood up, "That's okay; your friendship is enough." We pedaled back home, where mother and Bryce were loading up the car with gifts and a cake. I tried to ignore it, but the excitement was all over my face.

"Well, we're all loaded up, boys; let's go!" Bryce, Dell, Tony, and Chris all piled into the car, with mother up front and father driving. I climbed in the back as I was the smallest and could fit just about anywhere.

"Where are we going?" father asked, at which mother leaned over and whispered into his ear. "Oh?" he said, "that's a fine choice." As we drove up Main Street, the anticipation was eating away at me. We passed the Skate Palace, so not there; we passed Track's Go Karts, so not there; father drove to the end of town and finally pulled into Linguini's Pizza & Pasta, which was one of my favorite places to eat at. We were all pretty hungry too. We walked in through the front door and... SURPRISE! Someone yelled out. I was amazed. All my aunts and uncles, my cousins, and a handful of my friends were standing there. Even Mrs. Bell was there. I smiled my widest smile ever. We spent the rest of our time there visiting and playing games, then from out of the kitchen, here it came, a cake bristling with thirteen burning candlesticks, while everyone sang "Happy birthday" to me. When the singing came to a stop, it was my turn to blow out the candles. "Make your wish!" they all shouted. I paused for a moment to think about my wish. Do I wish for Buck, or do I wish to help Chris's dad, or do I wish for a shotgun? I only got one; I was confused more than ever now, so I closed my eyes and drew a big breath, and from my heart, made the wish for one of the things I wanted as I blew out all thirteen candles, and everyone clapped. It felt so good to have my best friend, Chris, right beside me. I sat at the table piled high with gifts. I felt so loved.

"Open ours first!" Tony and Dell shouted as they handed me a small yellow and blue striped box.

"Thanks," I said as I ripped open the package. A buck knife! I was so amazed. "This is so awesome!" I said, "thanks, guys." I now started tearing into the other gifts one after another—shirts, pants, shorts, some toys, and candy. I was in heaven, and then father came in with a longer box and sat down beside me. I thought to myself, could it be? Would it be? I slowly opened the corner, anticipation killing me, and then with one mighty jerk of the paper, it was revealed! Silence filled the room as tears streamed down my face. "Thank you, thank you, thank you!" I said as I stood up and threw my arms around him and mother both.

"Well, it's about time you have your own shotgun, boy!" I was so excited and could not wait to go shoot it.

"Can we go shooting tomorrow… please, please?"

Papa laughed and said, "Heck yes, we can." Just then, Bryce stepped up and handed me a bag, "Not much," he mumbled. I opened the bag; it was a small picture of a pack of wolves on a piece of wood that was cut sideways. "I made it for you," he said.

"Thanks, Bryce," I nodded, "I love it!" I was surprised that he would take the time to make this for me, as Bryce was always mean to me in so many ways. I honestly think this was the very first thing he had ever done that was nice, which made me appreciate it even more.

Everyone left as our family cleaned up the birthday mess and put all the gifts in the car. We headed back home, and as we pulled into the driveway, Mrs. Bell was sitting there on the front porch. I ran up to her, and she hugged me tightly, "There's one more present for you, my boy," she said as she pulled a small box from the pocket of her apron. It was wrapped in brown paper. I sat on the bench next to her as she handed it to me. She said, "Now, this gift comes with a lot of responsibility, mister, so be careful when opening it up." I thought to myself, what could it be in such a small package? I slowly unwrapped the paper as all of my family came in and gathered around to watch me open it up. Inside was a small box about five inches by five inches. I broke the tape that held the box lid closed and slowly lifted the top off to reveal a leather leash rolled up inside. All of a sudden, it hit me, and I could not hold my emotions in check any longer.

With tears rolling down my face, I looked at Mrs. Bell. "Really?" I breathed, and she nodded. "Yes indeed!" I looked up at Mom and Pop as if seeking their approval.

"You deserve it, son," Pop looked at me and said, "Why don't you look out back?"

"Buck!" I yelled with all the power in my lungs as I flew through the house to the back slider door, and there he was, with a big bow on his collar and all. I fell to my knees in front of him. "I love you, boy… so much!" as I hugged him around his neck, "you're family now, boy…" I looked back with tears and all to have my whole family and Chris standing behind me, all smiling at seeing me filled with such joy. I stood up, wiping the tears from my face, and ran to mother and father, "Thank you so much! How did you know about Buck?"

Father looked at me with one hand ruffling my hair, "We've known about him for some time now. Mrs. Bell told us everything." I ran to her and embraced her tightly.

"Thank you, Mrs. Bell! Thank you!" She was crying as well, and she said to me, "Now we still have a deal, eh? You have to help me with Buddy and take him for walks with Buck, okay?"

"No problem," I replied eagerly. "Thank you again, Mrs. Bell. I love you." We wound up that evening playing some cards and dominoes. It was nice to hang out as a family; even Bryce was having fun and being nice to me the whole night.

"Well, time for bed, boys. We're going to get up early

and go shooting." I smiled at pop as I got up from the couch, gave Mother a big hug, and thanked her for such a special day.

"Come on, Buck," I said as Chris and I headed to my room for the night. Soon I was tucked into bed, with Buck lying on the floor next to me. I was exhausted from such an adventurous day, It did not take long, and I was fast asleep.

Chapter Fourteen

I was up with the sun. Father was in the kitchen making us some coffee and sack lunches to take out shooting. "Come on, Buck," I said. Buck was lying in bed with Chris, with his head resting on Chris's legs. At my call, he raised his head and looked at me funny and then put his head back down as if he were ignoring me, so I reached over and nudged Chris. "Hey!" I said, "you going shooting today? Get up."

Chris woke up and looked up at me, and said, "Yes…" letting out a big yawn and stretching his arms out. Then he lay down again and put his arms around Buck, and hugged him tightly. "Good boy," he said to Buck as he lay there, cuddling my dog.

"Come on, Buck, let's go, boy," I said again. He got up slowly then, stretching his limbs on the floor, and then he followed me to the backyard to do his business. I opened up the door and let him out, and went back to see if I could help my dad. "Load up the guns in the back seat," he said to me, so I grabbed the bag of shells, and the three gun cases father had already set out for us. As I put the guns in the truck, Chris came out to help me and said to me, "My father used to do stuff like this when I was younger. He'd take my brother and me out shooting just about every other weekend; I'm actually a pretty good shot." We finished packing the truck and went back inside.

Mother was up now, and she fried some potatoes and eggs and bacon. "Can't go shooting on an empty stomach," she said to us all.

We sat down and ate, then Pop said, "Mount up, boys, let's go!"

As we headed for the door, I said, "Wait! I need to get Buck."

"Alright, go grab him."

"Come on, boy," I shouted as I opened the door, and Buck ran to the front door jumping up and down and wagging his tail. He was excited to be going with us. I opened up the front door, and Buck bolted for the truck. It was so funny to watch him as he ran around the truck and stopped by the tailgate, looking at me and then running around the truck again. It was so comical.

Father walked outside, saying, "I guess someone's excited; I think more than you boys are."

I looked at Pop, "We're excited too; we just don't have tails to wag." We all laughed as we piled into the truck. I hopped in next to Chris, and we were off.

While driving, Pop said, "You boys know it's actually dove and quail season, don't you?" I did not know that but was even more excited about going out now.

We drove for about an hour until pop swung the truck onto a dirt road. I knew right then that he was taking us to a place called Wiley's Well. It is a remote area in the desert that a lot of people did not know about, especially the outsiders who came here to hunt. We drove for about another twenty miles through the desert before father finally stopped.

"This looks like a good place," he said." The sun was just starting to rise over the top of the mountain, and you could see the dew sparkling on the leaves of the screw-bean trees and the sagebrush. The desert, to me, was home and a beautiful place to live. However, it is hotter than hell, and with not a lot of water around, you needed to be prepared, as father had taught me. The desert is beautiful, but you also have to show it some respect; many people do not, and mother nature claims them as her own.

We grabbed our canteens. I took my bird vest, a box of shells, and my new shotgun, and we all started walking. Buck stayed right beside me as if he knew what we were up to. We walked for about a hundred yards and came to a small brush-covered hill. Pop announced, "This looks like a good place for some dove hunting," and the birds were already starting to fly by, so we all huddled down to get ready.

"Here they come!" Chris whispered as the birds approached closer and closer, and at just the right moment, we popped up. Boom! Boom! Boom! went our guns. "Let's go pick them up!" Buck stayed by my side as we were walking.

I spotted two doves lying on the ground and said, "Go get them, boy!" Buck took off at a trot and picked up both birds at the same time and carried them back to me, and dropped them at my feet. Father looked over here, I said.

Father looked over and exclaimed, "Well, I'll be danged! I think Buck is going to earn his keep after all!" Pop leaned over and scratched him between the ears as Buck sat there looking up at him. The hunt continued for the next four hours until we all had our limit on birds. Mother would surely be pleased.

"Time to get on home, boys," Father said, so we all hauled our weary bones into the truck and started our journey back home. I was trying to stay awake, and I kept thinking about Chris and how I was going to get him and his father back together. He was a good friend and only wanted to be part of something real. With love and compassion from his father, I was sure God would help me figure something out.

We pulled up at the house at about 2 p.m., and Mother came out to greet us. How did you boys do?" she inquired.

"We all got our limit, so we better start cleaning some birds," I said triumphantly.

"Great!" Mother answered, "now get them to me, and I'll make some Spanish rice and dove breast." My mouth started watering because this was my second favorite meal, next to Buffalo sandwiches. Chris and I took the birds out back to the garbage cans and started plucking and preparing them birds. Doves were quite easy to clean; it was the quail that were the toughest ones. As we were working away at it, I said to Chris, "Have you been thinking about your dad at all?"

"Yes," he nodded, "but I don't miss him. I want to live with you guys forever." I laughed at him a bit, but I understood why. Our house was built on love and family values, but at the same time, there were rules and structure, and we were all held accountable for our actions. Mom or dad would not think twice about whipping my brothers or me when we deserved it. But Chris had not seen that part of the family, only the fun, good things. We finished up and took our bounty into the house for our mother. Chris yawned, "I'm going to go take a nap."

"Okay, I said. "I need to go to Mrs. Bell's house to clean the yard and take Buddy for a walk."

Mother looked at me and said, "Well, don't be gone all day, mister; dinner will be ready in a couple of hours."

I walked over to Mrs. Bell's house and knocked on the door. Buck was by my side. She may not have been home, as no one came to the door. I walked to the side fence, and Buddy was there to greet me. Buck and I went into the backyard, where I started cleaning up dog poop and took it to the trash. Then I took hold of the leash that she kept hanging by the back door. "Come on, Buddy, let's go for a walk." He was so excited to see Buck that he would hardly sit still as I put the leash on his collar. We walked down the street toward the old car wash. Walking two big dogs was not the easiest of tasks for a thirteen-year-old boy. Indeed, it seemed most of the time that these two dogs were giving me a walk. On our way, we passed Chris's house. As we got closer, I could see his dad sitting on the front porch with a cigarette in his hand. I stopped and paused for a second. I closed my eyes and asked God to give me the strength for what I was about to do next.

I slowly walked down his driveway. He sat and stared at me with every step I took closer to him. My final destination was to stand right in front of him. "What do you want, boy?" he demanded in a stern tone.

I replied, "I just want to help, that's all."

He looked away from me as he took a drag of his cigarette and said, "Haven't you done enough already?"

"No sir," I replied. "Chris loves you, but he fears you at the same time. He's the best friend I have ever had, and I would do anything for him."

"Well, ain't that grand?" he asked sarcastically. I looked him in the eye and said to him, "Yes, sir, it is grand. Haven't you ever had a best friend that you would do anything for?" He was silent and turned his head away from me and stared at the sky. I took a step closer to him and sat on the front step. He turned to look at me. He started to say something to me, but before he mentioned a word, I said to him, "I'll be your friend if you like; my name is Dustin," and I extended my hand to greet him.

As he looked at me, I could see the hurt in his eyes. Chris, not being here, was eating him up inside. My mother had a saying. You don't know what you have until it's gone. I think that applies to this situation. Now that he was gone, his father was missing him. Then he reached out and grabbed my hand, and we shook hands. I stood up and walked up the steps, and sat down next to him. He turned to me, and I could see a tear run down his cheek. I knew then he was hurting more than I had imagined. "Everything will be okay, I promise!"

He then grabbed me by both arms and pulled me close to him, and hugged me tighter than I have ever been hugged, "Tell my boy I'm sorry, and I love him," he sobbed as he broke down in tears. I knew then that he had hit rock bottom. Still in his embrace,

I said, "I will, and we'll get him back home soon. Maybe you can go to church with us Sunday if you like. A little Jesus never hurt anyone."

He surprised me with his reply, "You know I will; it's been a long time since I have been to God's house." We released our grasp and dabbed the tears from our eyes.

I stood up and said, "Well, I have to get going. It's getting late and Mom's fixing some good eats."

"Well, get home and maybe I will see you Sunday who

knows?" he said. I walked back home with a feeling in my heart like I had never felt before, one I could not explain, but it felt good. Well, something good had just happened. When I arrived at Mrs. Bell's house, I went to the side gate and put Buddy back in the yard. I then crossed through the front yard, walking over to my house.

As I passed by, I heard a voice, "So you're not going to stop by and say hi?" I looked over, and there was Mrs. Bell on the front porch, sitting there rocking in her chair.

"Well, of course, I am. I did not know you were home," I said as I walked in her direction. I sat down next to her and told her about my walk and what happened with Chris's dad.

She said to me, "God is listening to you for sure," but she still warned me to be careful. We talked for a few more minutes, and I headed back to the house with Buck. As I walked in, Chris was up from his nap, and everyone was in the living room watching TV. I took Buck to the backyard and then went back in to join them.

"Do you need any help, Mother?" I asked.

She said, "No, dinner will be ready in a few more minutes." I went and sat on the floor next to Chris and watched along with him. He had no idea of what had gone on between his dad and me, but I knew I needed to talk to mother about this after dinner.

Mother called out, "Time to eat, boys!" Getting up from the floor and couches, all of father and us made our way to the table.

"Smells good," Chris said to Mother.

She smiled, "Thanks." Mother had made Spanish rice with dove breast with all the trimmings. When we were finished eating, there were no leftovers, and everyone was stuffed. Our family accepted Chris; even my older brother Bryce treated him as our own. It was good for him to be a part of something real and to feel the love that our family had. After dinner, I asked my mother if she could talk with me. She followed me into my bedroom and sat at the foot of my bed. I explained to her what had happened today between Chris's father and myself. She looked at me and said, "You are a brave little man, aren't you? You really care for your friend Chris, don't you?"

"Yes, mother, I do."

"Well, what you did was dangerous, but I'm glad the outcome was good. You should probably let Chris know that his dad will be at church."

I smiled at her and nodded, "I will, Mom."

Chapter Fifteen

Sunday morning Chris and I were up early. We sat on the couch, eating a bowl of cereal and watching cartoons. I looked at Chris and said, "Oh, I forgot to tell you something. Your father is going to go to church with us today."

His eyes grew twice their size, "No way!" he exclaimed, "but how do you know this?" Then I told Chris the story. I made it very clear to him that his father did love him a lot and was sorry for the way he had treated him. There were a lot of things his father was going through, "He missed your mom, and because you remind him of her, he took his anger out on you." I told Chris that his father had hit rock bottom.

"But losing you made him realize that he can't go on treating you like that."

Chris looked up at me with tears rolling down his cheeks, "I love my dad too, but I can't go back unless I'm sure he won't beat me anymore." I guess it all made sense to him as he thanked me. I assured him that we would not let him go home and be treated like that, and he wiped the tears from his face. By then, mother was up.

"You boys going to church today?"

"Yes, ma'am," I replied as Chris and I got up to go to our room to change into our Sunday clothes. We all squeezed into the car, and soon we were on our way. We arrived a bit early. I did not know why, but mother called me to go with her as the others waited in the foyer. Our Bishop was an honest, loving man. Bishop Smith was a soft-spoken man with a big heart; he was also a big man at that.

Mother took me to his office, where he sat reading the scripture. "Come on in," he said to Mother and me. We entered his office, and mother closed the door behind us. You could see the concern on Bishop Smith's face; knowing that the door was closed, he sensed this must be a big deal to require such privacy. Mother told him the story of Chris and me and how we had become friends, and how he came to live with us.

"Dustin," Bishop Smith said to me, "What do you have to say about this?" I looked at him, and tears wet my cheek,

"Well," I said, "I invited Chris's dad to church today so as to heal his heart and bring the two of them closer to each other and to God as well. He is not a bad man at all; it's just that he misses his wife and their life together. I know he loves his son and his son loves him back, but he is angry that his wife has left him.

"You know his wife passed last year." Bishop Smith said to me,

"Yes, they came to church every week, and they seemed to be a happy and fruitful family. Well, I'm very glad that you got him to come today, as the missionaries have been to his house several times only to be turned away in anger. God does work in mysterious ways, for sure. Thanks for bringing this to my attention."

Bishop Smith extended his hand to me, and as we shook, he said, "You are a good friend and turning into a good man like your father." Those words made me happier than ever because all I wanted was to be just like my dad. I guess I was on the right track.

The church was filling up, and as we entered the main chapel, there was Chris' father sitting in the second to last row. Chris walked up to him and put his arms around his father as his father did to him. "I love you, son," he muttered with broken words.

"I love you too, Dad," Chris replied. We all sat down next to him in the pews, with Chris on one side of his father and me on the other, beside my mother and father, followed by Dell, Bryce, and Tony. My heart was happy to see the reunion of a father and his son. I looked over at Mother, and she had tears in her eyes. Bishop Smith took his place at the podium and offered the opening prayer, followed by a song. Then a quietness filled the room as he began to speak.

"You know I had this wonderful sermon planned for today, but as I look at the congregation today, filled with all you mothers and fathers and families, I want to talk about a father's love for his son and his love for us." I thought it was pretty awesome that Bishop Smith would change his sermon to fit the needs of the one family that needed it the most. I looked over to see Chris reach out and grab his dad's hand. As tears fell from his father's face, I leaned across and handed him my handkerchief, which he took and thanked me. You could see his heart swell from the words of Bishop Smith, as did the hearts of our whole entire family. Even my father had to dry his eyes from the emotional speech that filled our ears. After the sermon was over, we sat there and waited for all to leave the room. Bishop Smith stood by the door to thank each and every person for coming. We stood up and made our way toward him.

"Chris," the bishop said, "I'm so glad you and your father came to rejoice with us today!" He extended his hand to Chris and his father, and when he took Chris's father's hand, he said, "especially you, Charles!" That was Chris's father's name. "You are welcome here anytime, and we are glad to have you back with your family." Chris's father thanked Bishop Smith, and we all walked out the door. I stopped for a second to tell the bishop how much I liked his sermon. "Well, sometimes the right words need to be said to bring us closer together as a family," he answered.

I walked over to where Mother and Charles were talking. "I'd love it if you would come for dinner tonight," Mother said.

"I've got something to do," Charles said.

Father stepped up and extended his hand, and said, "We won't take no for an answer! You know those things can wait for another day."

Charles looked my father in the eye and said, "I'll be there." They shook hands, and although they never apologized to each other, I could tell all was forgiven, even without words. We all made our way home then. I was sure mother was going to fix one of her best Sunday meals. We arrived home, where Chris and I had changed out of our Sunday clothes. I let Mother know that I needed to take Buck and Buddy for their walk.

"Okay," Mother said, "but don't be very long." We walked next door and met Mrs. Bell. I introduced Chris to her, and they sat and chatted while I rounded up Buddy and was ready to head out.

"Come on, Buck!" He took the lead as always; he just had to be the dog in front. I handed Buck to Chris to walk since they already had a special bond with each other, and being bigger, Chris could control him better than I. We walked to the city park, where we took the dogs off the leash and tossed a stick for them.

Chris looked at me and said, "Hey, I want to thank you for what you did today. I think my father is better now."

"Yes," I replied, "I think so too."

"You know," he continued, "it's my birthday tomorrow, too."

"Wow!" I exclaimed, "I had no idea! Well, you could not ask for a better present than you being back with your dad."

"That is true," he said. I wanted to do more for Chris, but I did not know what at the time. We continued to toss the stick for the dogs. I'd toss the stick for Buddy, and he'd bring it back to me; then, I would toss the stick for Buck, and he'd bring it back to Chris. This kind of made me a little sad because he was my dog, but he seemed to have more of an attachment to Chris. I watched as Chris bent down how Buck would lick his face furiously. He was so excited that Chris was here. It was getting late, so we stopped by and dropped Buddy off at Mrs. Bell's house first, then headed back to mine.

Mother and father were there sitting in the living room, so mother said, "Chris, are you ready to go back home?"

He smiled and said, "Yes." You could tell that Chris really loved his father, just like I loved mine.

The doorbell rang, I ran to the door and opened it up, and there stood Chris's father. Come on in; I invited him.

As he walked in, he stopped for a second and sniffed the air, "Sure does smell good," he stated. He reached up and took his hat off and grasped it with both hands in a humbling way; I could tell he was pretty nervous. Father walked in and almost shoved me out of the way to greet our guest.

Father then said to Charles, "Hey, while they are fixing dinner, why don't you and I go hang out in the garage?"

As we all started to walk out the back door to the garage, Mother called out to me, "Dustin?" Mother asked.

"Yes," I replied as I poked my head back in the door.

"Why don't you stay here and help me with dinner,"

"But, Mom," I exclaimed. She smiled back at me as I came back inside with my head hung low. I did not know it at the time, but Chris' father and mine both hit it off, little did any of us know, but Charles loved to fish and so did my father, so after dinner, the stories didn't stop. I think my father found a new lifelong buddy that night.

We all sat down at the table for another great meal my mother had made. As we sat down, I asked Mother if I could bless the food; she smiled and said that we should offer one of our guests the opportunity to bless the food. Mother looked up at Charles. "Would you do the honors, Charles," she asked.

Silence filled the room, and he said, "You know it's been a very long time for me, but if you don't mind, I'd love to give it my best." I reached my hand out to Charles as he did to Chris until we all formed a chain around the table.

Charles starts out, "Our dear father in heaven, We thank you, Lord, for this bounty of food; please bless this food to strengthen our bodies. Lord, thank you so much for this family, thank you for bringing them into our lives, and thank you again for my son. I know I have done wrong, dear Lord. Please forgive me for my past. Thanks again for the sacrifice that you have made for us all. For these things, we pray for in Jesus' name. Amen." After dinner, we played some Dominoes and told old stories, and laughed until it was late. Charles got up from the table and said, "Well, I think I've overstayed my welcome. Chris, are you ready to go?" Chris looked up and asked if he could stay one more night. Charles laughed and said, "Sure, but I think you are just getting used to this good cooking," we laughed.

The next morning we then gathered up Chris' belongings and got in the car to head to Chris' house. As we pulled into the driveway, his father was standing out front. I don't think the car had even stopped yet when Chris jumped out and ran as fast as he could and jumped into his father's arms. My mother pulled out a handkerchief and dabbed at the tears in her eyes. Mother and Father stayed in the car as I got out of the car to take Chris' clothes to his house. I handed the bag of clothes to Chris, and he went inside.

His father got down on both knees to look at me eye to eye. "I want to tell you again, thanks for bringing my boy back and healing this family. You are a courageous young man!" He put his arms around me and hugged me, "Thank you so much," he whispered into my ear.

I went back to the car and yelled out to Chris, "I'll see you tomorrow, okay?" They both stood on the porch and waved to us as we pulled out of the driveway. It was so wonderful to see Chris standing there with his father's arm around him. It made my heart feel good; even my dad was touched by this emotional moment. He tried to hide it, but you could see it on his face.

"Ice cream, anyone?" he asked so as to change the mood.

Mother said, "Isn't it a little early for that?"

"It's never too early for ice cream!" he retorted, and we stopped at the local ice cream store for some vanilla cones before driving back home.

Chapter Sixteen

Morning dawned early, and the house seemed quiet without Chris there. Buck lay in the spot where Chris had slept, and I could see that he was missed. "Come on," I said, "let's go," but he just lay there. I ignored him then and went on with my morning. When it was about eleven o'clock, and Buck still had not come out of the bedroom, I went to the room, and he was still in the same spot, sulking from the absence of Chris. I sat down beside him, petting his head. "Don't worry, boy, we'll see him today." He lifted his head and looked at me, and let out a deep breath as if he were relieved by my words. I thought to myself that maybe there was something more to Buck than we all saw, It was Buck that brought me closer to Chris. If it wasn't for that day on the canal where Buck had taken Chris's shoe, none of this would have ever happened.

"Come on, Buck," I pulled on his collar and walked him to the backyard as I was walking out the door.

Mother called out, "Dustin, you have a phone call!" I took the receiver from her hand. It was Chris.

"Hey, we're having cake and ice cream at the park today at one o'clock. Can you make it?" I looked over at Mom and asked if it was okay.

"Yes, we'll be there," I said. He replied back, can you bring Buck too, I Laughed out loud and said of course as I hung up the phone. I then sat down with my mother and had some breakfast.

"Do you need to bring a gift?" she asked me. I said,

"Well, he told me not to, but I have an idea of something."

I spent the next few hours making a card for him until about twelve thirty came along, and Mother, Father, Buck, and I all got into the car and headed to the park. There were not a lot of people there when we got out of the car. Buck pulled the leash right out of my hands and ran as fast as he could to Chris, jumping up on the boy and knocking him down. Chris was laughing out loud, and I think Buck was just as happy.

"Glad you could make it," his father said to us. There were about three or four other kids there, mostly from school and some relatives. We sang "Happy birthday" and ate cake and ice cream. Chris was so excited as he sat and started opening the gifts, mostly a few video games and some clothes, and his father said, "I got one more for you, buddy." He walked to his truck and pulled out a box from behind the seat, and handed it to Chris. "I hope you like it," he said to him. Chris tore open the paper faster than I'd ever seen, and we were all surprised to see when he opened the box that it was a new twelve-gauge shotgun.

Chris flew from his seat and ran to his father, hugging him as tight as ever, saying over and over, "Thank you, thank you, thank you!" Now we can all go shooting together Chris exclaimed.

We finished our ice cream and cake, then mother and I helped to clean up some of the mess. Most of the other guests had already left when I looked over at Chris and his father and announced, "Wait. I've got one more gift for you." All eyes were on me as I walked up to Chris. Buck was standing right beside me. I slowly pulled my hand out of my right pocket and extended it out to Chris; both our eyes filled with tears. I said to him, "Chris, he needs you more than I need him." He looked over at this father, who nodded his head in approval, then he took the leash out of my hand and dropped down on his knees with both his arms around Buck. The tears fell from his face to the ground, and he looked up at me in disbelief.

This was the hardest thing I have ever had to do, giving away something that I loved so much. But I knew in my heart that this was what God wanted. I could feel deep inside my soul. Chris then pulled me to the ground, where we all three embraced in a hug, "You're the best friend anyone could ever have," Chris said to me.

Those words had so much meaning to me that day, and I have never forgotten them. Have faith and cherish the ones around you, your friends and your family, making new friends even out of a stranger and doing good to others.

If we all take the time to do something nice for someone each and every day without asking for anything in return but only for the feeling of doing something good, just think how much better the world would be. Thinking back to that day, I blew out my candles and made that wish. God works in mysterious ways is a hundred percent true. I got my shotgun and my dog, but the only thing I truly wished for was for Chris to be reunited with his father.

THE END

www.ingramcontent.com/pod-product-compliance
Lightning Source LLC
Chambersburg PA
CBHW052140220626
47052CB00005B/1136